THE PATROL

BY

ADRIAN M. HURTADO

ISBN: 978-1-969865-17-6 (sc)
ISBN: 978-1-969865-18-3 (e)

Rev. date: 010/06/2025

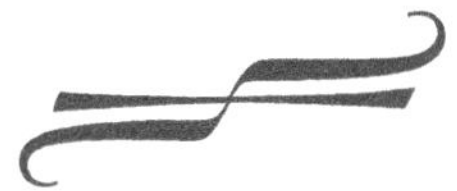

Dedicated to the American veteran,
all races, creeds, colors, and genders

Get up you men," the sergeant said,
"your names are on the roll.
You twelve have just been volunteered
for the Night Patrol.

Don't sneer at me, I didn't plan
this job you have to do.
Besides, I'm on the Captain's list.
I'm going with you, too.

So grab your weapons and your gear
and fix a light field pack.
You have twenty minutes, men,
then meet me out in back."

Twelve men begin to move about
like twelve weary mutes.
Silently they dress themselves
and lace their jungle boots.

One man stands to go outside
and grabs his M-16.
"I hope we don't fight," he remarks.
"I hate to clean this thing."

"Hurry up men, get out back.
This is no Sunday stroll.
If we are any slower,
we'd be the Dawn Patrol

Thirteen men all saddled up
move out from the camp.
They leave behind the
light and warmth
and enter dark and damp.

They cross the camp perimeter
and now they're on their own.
Thirteen men together,
Yet, thirteen men alone.

Three clicks out, their instincts say
that something isn't right.
A flare goes up and thirteen men
are captured in its light.

Shots ring out! The air is filled
with screams of fear and pain.
A soldier crumbles to the ground
to never move again.

Another soldier grabs his chest,
another grabs his head.
"Take cover now", the
sergeant screams,
"or you'll all be dead!"

The fighting lasts what
seems like hours,
and then the night is still.
How many of the thirteen live?
How many did they kill?

Two days later, back at camp
Commanders check the roll.
But thirteen men are missing still,
now dubbed the Lost Patrol.